EVE HALLOWS
AND THE
BOOK OF SHRIEKS

Available October 2011

Robert Gray

This book is a work of fiction. Names, characters, places, and incidents are either a product of the author's imagination or are used fictitiously. Any resemblance to actual events, locales, or persons, living or dead, is entirely coincidental.

ISBN-13: 978-1463765668
ISBN-10: 1463765665

Cover Art Design by Shaun Lindow

For Theresa,
a most horrible daughter

CONTENTS

ONE
THE ADORABLE NEWS

Around midnight, the hissing and growling noises began echoing through the halls. I heard whispers, too. Muddled at first, but once they got closer, I realized they were talking about me.

Do you think she's still upset?

Of course she is.

Maybe I should talk to her?

No, you'll just make it worse. I'll do it.

Good idea.

I didn't want to talk to either of them, because, yes, I was still upset. I sat up on my bed, grabbed my journal off the nightstand, and pretended to act busy. I'd already written my entry for the night, so I began tracing the letters again and managed to fatten the first sentence considerably when the old wooden floor in my bedroom creaked. I sighed. They never could take a hint.

1

Even though I had my back to her, I knew she was right behind me. I could hear soft rattling and feel little breaths breaking against the back of my neck.

When I glanced up, a tangle of shiny black snakes dripped into my face.

"Mom! Hel*lo*! A little privacy please," I said, pushing the snakes away.

Mom sat next to me on my bed, her golden eyes examining the words in my journal. "What are you writing about?"

"Nothing important. Just my life. Or what's left of it, at least."

Mom, still eyeing my *private* journal, shook her head. "You're so dramatic, Eve. I don't think moving to a new town will put you in any danger."

I snapped my journal shut and tossed it on the bed. "How do you know? Maybe when we get there the humans will have pitchforks and torches and—"

"You read too many stories, sweetheart. It's not like that."

"That's not what Sally says. She says that humans hunt monsters for fun."

"You shouldn't listen to Sally. She's a werewolf, and humans used to hunt them because they kept eating the farmers' animals. Humans a fine species, once you get to know them."

"A fine species? You're kidding, right? What about all those stories you told us about turning humans into stone?"

"Petrified the humans," Mom corrected. "Turning to stone sounds so first century. Besides, it wasn't because I didn't like the humans. We just didn't see eye to eye." She snickered at her own joke, while I rolled my eyes. Like I haven't heard that one before.

Nowadays Mom wore special contacts or sunglasses to protect us from being *petrified*. Sometimes she'd lose a contact or her glasses would drop from her eyes, which was why our backyard overflowed with statues. But these were only accidents. She never petrified anything out of anger, at least not since she met Dad.

"Things have changed since those days," Mom added. "Humans are much more civilized than they used to be. They can be trusted now."

Me trust a human? Ha!

Okay, so I am a human. But in my defense, I haven't seen another one since being dumped off at my family's doorstep when I was a baby. No way could I ever trust a species that abandons their children.

"And a new school. With humans! It's not fair. You're not making Sam go to school."

Mom slipped an arm around me, and some of her snake hair cuddled around my neck, which normally cheered me up the way they kissed my face and all, but I wasn't in the mood today. Today, it was going to take a whole lot more to cheer me up. Like for starters, Mom and Dad saying they made a *huge* mistake, and that we were staying right here in Gravesville, and that I should unpack my stuff right away and forget they ever came up with this ridiculous idea in the first place.

"Sweetheart, your brother's a ghoul. He's a bit—"

"Gross?"

3

"—*Different* from the humans. He wouldn't fit in. I'm going to homeschool him myself."

"Why can't I be homeschooled then?"

Mom's golden eyes drifted to the floor, and her snakes went limp. "Because ... Well, sweetheart, your father and I decided it would be good for you to learn more about your heritage."

"Oh! I am *so* not one of them! They're like wild beasts! With pitchforks! And torches!"

"You know we're only trying to do what's best for everyone."

"Then let's stay here. That's what's best for everyone."

As Mom stood, her snakes curled up around each other and slid back into a ponytail. "You don't understand, Eve. Things are different now," she said and left me alone to brood over what *that* was supposed to mean.

What was different? And wasn't there a certain look on Mom's face, one that said she didn't want to leave, either?

My parents were keeping secrets from us. I was sure of it. This whole moving-to-the-human-world nonsense was just too weird.

I already felt homesick, and we hadn't left yet. I opened up my curtains and stared out my window, which faced the sprawling graveyard. If it's one thing Gravesville is known for, it's the graveyard. It goes on and on, rolling up a gloomy hill and disappearing in the mist and blackness beyond.

Most monsters wished for gravefront property, and my parents expected me to leave this all behind? They might as well have ripped out my soul and fed it to the corpse-sucking demons in the Waste Lands. Even that would've been an improvement.

Tonight, the graveyard was packed with tourists. We get a lot of them this time of year—zombies from up north. They were the rudest, most annoying creatures. And that whole brain-eating thing? I don't care where you live, that's just poor manners. Not to mention, they were having so much fun out there in the graveyard, which made me dislike them even more. I wanted to be out there, too.

I liked to fog surf—you know, grab a possessed board, wait for a wave of mist to creep in and ride it out. If I were in the graveyard right now, that's what I'd be doing.

But why bother? I'd have to leave the graveyard behind soon enough. I was better off staying inside and getting used to being miserable, which did have some benefits. For example, misery allowed me to feel sorry for myself, which is a necessity when you're fourteen, even though my parents didn't seem to understand that. Mom and Dad thought it was a human problem, something in my blood. They made it sound like the rest of my deformities, if you ask me, like having straight brown hair instead of Mom's gorgeous black snakes, or not being able to shape shift like Dad, or ooze goo through my skin when I got excited like my brother Sam.

But I had the heart of a monster. That much I knew. And regardless of what species I belonged to, I belonged here.

I heard four little feet tap into my room. "Hey, Wolf. How's my good boy doing tonight?"

He grunted and then poked my ankle with his snout. I rubbed him in that place behind the ear he loved so much, which caused his little foot to tap spastically against the wood floor.

"What do you think about the Move?"

Another grunt followed by two snorts. I couldn't agree more.

Wolf was a were-pig. At least that's what the goblin who sold him to us had said. He also said it would take a few years before Wolf showed his wolfish side. It was going on three years, and Wolf still hasn't shown the slightest bit of interest in a full moon, or any other moon. It was okay, though. I liked him better this way, because he was more like me. We were both pink skinned. We were both different.

But there I go ... getting off track again. Back to the move.

This whole mess started last week, on one of those horrible stormy nights where it seemed nothing could go wrong. That evening, when Dad got home from work, he looked traumatized, like he'd just seen a human. He rushed Mom upstairs into their bedroom and slammed the door shut. Sam and I knew something was wrong, so we followed them and pressed our ears to their door. We didn't hear much, mostly because Sam's husky breathing kept getting in the way, and all we learned from their conversation was that we were moving.

The next day, Mom and Dad were out shopping for a new house. It happened that fast. But the real shocker was that we were moving to a place called Poke-A-Nose, Pencil-vania, which sounded weird. And annoying.

My parents had showed us a picture of the new house. Oh, my Jack, it looked boring! And poor Sam, he must've leaked a bucket of goo when Dad told him the closest graveyard was five miles away. A ghoul without a graveyard is like a swamp creature without a swamp.

At least my parents agreed not to sell our castle. It had been in the family for over six hundred years, and most of the family—even though they were ghosts—still lived here. They would be devastated if they lost their haunt. So Dad asked Grandma and Grandpa to watch the house while we were gone. That was when I knew the move was final, because under any other circumstance Dad would never let his parents watch the castle. My grandparents could get a bit *wild* when not supervised.

I still had some more stuff to pack, last minute items that had no business being in a box. There was my *Book of Spells*. (I didn't know a lick of magic, but the spells were like poetry, and I enjoyed reading them.) And there were my voodoo baby dolls, which I'd been collecting since I was three. Next semester, my school's going to dedicate two full classes on voodoo, a history course, and a practical applications course. I finally would get the chance to use my voodoo baby dolls, but no*oo*. I get to go to school with humans instead. The excitement!

And the good news didn't stop there, because I also learned we were traveling to the Poke-A-Nose by ship. For ten days! Until last week all travel into the human world had been done through portals, but ever since the murders began, URNS—the Undead, Reanimated, and Nocturnal Services—decided to ban all portal travel.

I needed a drink. This was too upsetting.

"Hey, freak," Sam said as I entered the kitchen. He sounded so depressed, and he looked it, too. His ears doubled over, and his scales had almost no sheen, as if he were shedding.

I grabbed myself a mug of hot pumpkin—my all-time favorite drink—and offered one to Sam. It was his favorite, too, but he said he didn't want one, and he hunched over more than normal and sighed, which I knew was his pathetic attempt to get me to make him feel better.

It worked.

"So I heard the nearest graveyard is like five miles away from our new house."

Sam's ears twitched as if swatting at flies. "Yeah. And did you hear what else?"

"What?"

"There's only dead people at the graveyard."

This was so shocking I almost dropped my drink. "Are you kidding me? What kind of sanity is this?"

Sam looked ready to cry. I was ready to sob myself! But I had to be strong for both of us, me being the older sister and all.

"Maybe we can reanimate some of the corpses," I suggested. "I have my spell book."

"You promise?"

"Absolutely." I felt adorable lying like this, but Sam looked so pathetic before and now he was smiling. Besides, maybe it would work ...

Better yet, maybe he would forget the whole thing.

The first gray hint of morning peeked through my window as I lay sleepless on my bed, watching the shadows wander across the ceiling. I couldn't stop thinking about The Move and how it was going to ruin my life.

Dad growled from somewhere downstairs. Curious, I opened my door and listened. Mom and Dad were arguing about something, but I couldn't quite hear. As I crept down the hall, I heard Dad's rumbling snarl again. He must be in his gargoyle form, or maybe a hellhound. I think I mentioned my dad was a shapeshifter. He could turn into almost anything, but preferred animals when he was upset. Otherwise, he mostly stayed in his human form, because— he often joked—he wanted to be like me when he grew up. In reality, he did it so I wouldn't be the only human in Gravesville, and I loved him for it.

Dad worked for URNS, in the Watchers Division, what I liked to call the Secret Spy Lab. Dad didn't do much spying these days. He mostly catalogued information brought to him by other spies. Not the most exciting position, if you ask me, but he did come home with a lot of cool stuff, like my spell book, which had to be super rare, because I'd never seen another one like it.

My parents' conversation had taken on a secretive hushy tone—which are the ones I liked to eavesdrop on the most—and I hurried down the stairs, fearing I might miss something. I'd forgotten how loud the steps creaked until Mom and Dad shushed each other.

I crouched below the railing and held my breath. My parents stayed silent for a long time, probably trying to decide if they heard someone listening to them. Fortunately, this place made all sorts of noises at night—one of the benefits of living in a haunted castle. Even better, Uncle Mervin floated by with a book tucked under his arm, complaining to himself about how he couldn't get any reading done with all that ruckus, and he poofed through the wall in search of a quieter location.

I eased out the breath that'd been burning up in my chest and waited for my parents to start talking again.

"Pizza?" Mom whispered. "What do you know about pizza?"

"Absolutely nothing, but that's what they gave me. The place is called Ghoulicious Pizza."

"You can turn into anything, and they want you to manage a pizza place?"

"They told me it was low-key, and that every human loves pizza, so chances are they won't suspect anything."

"And the murders?"

Hold on. Now this was getting interesting. The murders have been all over the news for the last few months. In school, the only thing we talked about more than the murders was the super-cool rock band the Ghastly Brothers—Nick Ghastly is perfectly horrible, by the way, I don't care what Sally says.

Did my dad know who had been committing these murders? I stretched so far over the railing to listen that I nearly tipped over the side.

"Four more this week. A family of vamps. Can you believe it? The youngest was a baby, only 120 years old."

"How adorable! And they have no idea who's behind this?"

Dad must've shaken his head, because I didn't hear him say anything. They were being even quieter now, which, of course, made me more interested. I didn't have a choice. You don't toss a word like *murder* up in the air and wait for it to hit the ground. I inched my way down the stairs and would've made it the whole way, too, if not for that second-to-last step, which creaked so loud under my weight. It sounded like a ten-pound toad!

I froze. On came the lights and out popped Dad's heads. He was shifting from a two-headed gargoyle into his human form as he approached me.

"Eve? What are you doing up so late?"

I couldn't say spying, so I said the first thing that popped into my mind. "I guess I—er—was sleepwalking."

"Sleepwalking?" That was Mom's voice, all loaded with sarcasm.

"Yeah. I was dreaming about the humans again, and they were chasing me with their torches and pitchforks yelling DEMON GIRL! GET HER! And the next thing I know I'm standing on the steps and—"

"You were spying on us," Mom said flatly.

"And I was spying on you," I agreed.

Dad sighed. "Oh, for Jack's sake. How long have you been on the steps?"

"A couple of minutes. I only heard about pizza. I like the name Ghoulicious, by the way. Oh, and there was that little thing about murder ..."

"That's nonsense," Mom said, but her snakes squirmed and snapped, suggesting the opposite.

"Mom, your snakes are upset. What gives?"

"There are big problems going on, sweetheart," she said. "Problems you couldn't possibly understand. It's best that we leave, and it's best that we don't discuss them."

"I heard you two talking about a murdered vamp family. Are we moving because you're worried we'll be next?"

Dad threw up his hands in surrender. "Guess she understands the problem about as well as we do."

I was proud of myself for putting two and two together. I could be pretty smart when I wanted to be, even for a human.

"But you need to understand this is for your safety," Dad added. "It's just temporary until they find out who's responsible for those hideous crimes."

"You could've told me this earlier. I wouldn't have complained about The Move so much." Which was almost true. The idea of going into hiding excited me, like we were secret agents in some thriller novel—trying to unmask the criminal mind in *The Murders of Gravesville*. Soon to be in bookstores everywhere.

And feeling like a secret agent, I added, "So what clues do we have?"

"Clues?" Mom said. Her snakes snickered at me.

"I shouldn't be showing you this, but there is one clue. The killers have been leaving these." Dad pulled a card from his pocket and held it up for me and Mom to see.

It looked like ... a business card? Where's the originality in that? Centered on the card in a boldface type were two little words: THE SOURCE.

"Who's The Source?" I asked.

Dad shrugged. "No one knows for sure, but we think it's a group."

"Why would URNS suspect a group?" Mom asked. She grabbed the card, flipped it over, and then gave a puzzled look. Besides those two words, the card was blank.

Dad's face turned grim, like he just swallowed a witch's mucky brew. "The murders happened too fast. There's no way one creature could've done them."

"Some monsters are pretty fast," I offered.

"These murders weren't committed by any monster," Dad said. "That much we know."

"Then who?"

"Humans did it."

TWO

GOODBYE, GRAVESVILLE

I stared at my parents. For once, I was speechless, and it took me a while to recover from what my dad had just said. Humans? Was this some adorable joke?

"Can somebody *please* tell me why we're going to live with the same creatures that are trying to kill us?"

"I volunteered. They needed someone on the inside to spy out the area. URNS has strong evidence that suggests The Source's headquarters are in Pencil-vania."

"YOU WHAT!" I looked to Mom for support and got none.

"I did it to protect us. Think about it: The Source isn't going to try anything near where they live. But if we're here ..." He let the thought hang for a moment. "Some of those murdered were undercover operatives in URNS." Dad rubbed at his tired eyes, as if trying to erase certain images from his memory. "The Source is looking for something, and they are knocking off URNS employees to find it."

"But what if the killers go to my school?" A mean trick, sure, but if it got me out of going to school with humans, then I'd use it.

"Nice try, but The Source isn't after humans," Mom said.

"Maybe they'll kidnap me and use me as bait."

"Yeah, and maybe Wolf will turn into a wolf someday," Dad said.

I spent the next afternoon saying goodbye to Gravesville, which wasn't much time at all. Sure, I'd known about The Move for a week—and in rock star fashion I had like several farewell tours before most everyone I knew was good and sick of saying goodbye to me—but even if my parents had given me a year, it still wouldn't have been enough time. I have a hard time with goodbyes, simple as that. I guess it was all part of that human deformity my parents were certain I had.

But deformity or not, I wanted everyone to know I'd be leaving soon, and, more importantly, I wanted everyone to feel sorry for me.

The only monsters who still seemed to care about The Move were my best friends Sally, Pia, and Stephinica. They were werewolves ... well, almost werewolves. They were at that awkward pre-wolf stage, which meant an over abundance of baby fur covered their shoulders and backs. They wouldn't become actual werewolves until they turned sixteen. Once they make a full transformation, all that extra fur disappears while in their human form, which was good, I guess, because they would look more like me. But sometimes I worry that once they turn, they won't want to be friends with me any more, and it seemed every time we got together they had a little more fur, especially Sally, who now had long blonde curls running down her entire back. She was so pretty.

We agreed to meet over at the Ogopogo Grill for lunch. The Grill overlooked Lake Ogopogo, where the sea creature of the same name could often be seen scaring away zombie tourists who thought the monster was a myth.

I found an empty table near the window, so I sat there and stared out at the lake. The sea creature wasn't around, though there were plenty of doubtful zombies crowded around the edge of the water. This should be good.

Inside the restaurant, goblin workers hung strings of eyeballs along the wooden beams in preparation for Halloween. I realized then that I wouldn't be home for the holiday, which didn't help my mood any.

In Gravesville, Halloween wasn't just a holiday, it was a the single most important event of the year. The festivals lasted for weeks, and the preparation ran year round. And I was going to miss it for the first time in my life.

I was on the verge of screaming, or crying, or some combination of both, when I saw my three best friends walk in.

Sally didn't waste a moment, her being the reigning gossip queen of Gravesville. "Did you hear there was another death? A family of vamps. We went to school with one of them. I think her name was Lacy or Nancy or something like that."

I'd already known about the murders, but Dad told me not to tell anyone, especially Sally. Everyone knew that she-wolf could not keep a secret. "Really? That's adorable!"

"Yeah," Pia added. "It's probably a good thing you're leaving, Eve. At least you won't have to worry about being murdered. Wait! What am I talking about? You don't have to worry, anyway. You're not even a monster."

"You idiot." Stephinica raised her hand to smack Pia on the back of the head.

"What?" Pia scooted her chair out of Stephinica's reach. "What did I say? She's not a monster. That's a good thing for her, right?"

"You'll always be a monster to us," Sally said.

I guess I looked upset, but I wasn't. Well, not because they didn't consider me a monster—I had gotten used to that. It was because of what my dad had told me, how the killers were human, like me. I was safe because I was one of them, and that made me mad.

"So I heard that Kimberly Glastone and her family are moving, too. And the Sheldings next to me put their house up for sale, so you're not alone, Eve," Sally said. "I think they're crossing the border into zombie territory." She shrugged. "Guess they think living next to brain eaters is better than being killed."

"It's a tossup," Pia said.

"Zombies can't be any worse than humans," I said, and we all laughed. It felt good to be with my friends.

17

The waitress strolled over to us. She appeared almost human, except she had a giant stomach mouth instead of the under-the-nose variety. I'm always one to compliment good fashion sense, so I told her I liked the way her lipstick matched her belly shirt.

She thanked me and asked, "Can I start you girls off with something to drink?"

"I think this calls for four pumpkin sodas," Sally announced.

We all agreed. That was my second favorite drink next to hot pumpkin.

"So you're really taking a boat to the human world?" Pia asked after the waitress left.

"Don't remind me," I muttered. "Turns out we aren't allowed to travel by portal because ..." and I let that hang, too. It might also be Top Secret information.

"Yeah, I think URNS closed the portals when the murders started. I don't know why. Probably to keep the humans out, I guess," Sally said.

"But they can't stop *all* portal travel," Pia argued. "They'd have to confiscate every key and keep an agent at every tombstone."

"URNS doesn't need to worry about the tombstones, because you can't travel through one without a portal key. Besides, my mom told me each key is registered with URNS, so they have a good idea of who owns a key. They can even tell when one is used. If URNS catches anyone using a key, they're gonna be arrested for murder." Stephinica said. Her mom worked for URNS, too. I thought I should pull her aside and compare notes, but changed my mind when our frosty mugs of pumpkin soda arrived.

Sally raised her mug first. "To friends," she said.

"To friends," we agreed.

And as we clinked our mugs together, old Ogopogo burst from the water and thrashed at the terrified zombies, who ran and screamed for safety. Whoever said zombies were slow has obviously never seen one chased by a sea creature.

Good times ... Good times.

After much goodbye saying and promising that we would write to each other every day—Pia even promised to write to Sally even though Pia wasn't moving anywhere, and she lived three houses down from Sally—I headed downtown to where all my haunts were. There was the Bobbing Bones, which served the best hot pumpkin this side of Gravesville; Hottentots, my favorite clothing store; and Books & Brimstone, which had the new *Nightmare Books* on display in the front window. The series was loosely based on the legend of how monsters were created, and I've been salivating over the release for months. Too bad I spent the last of my money at Ogopogo Grill.

I forced myself away from the window, and continued on. Next to the book store was Jack o' Salon, where pumpkin heads could get new facial expressions to fit their mood—nothing worse than mad jack-o'lanterns forced to wear smiles all day. Then I passed my all-time favorite eatery, Treats n' Treats, an all-you-can eat candy buffet.

I wanted to spend hours in each place, but glancing at the clock above Blood Bank, I noticed I only had another hour before I needed to be home, so I patted the stone wall of Treats n' Treats and whispered goodbye.

A silky fog rolled in over the graveyard as I headed for home, and I leaned against the iron bars and savored the view. If I had my possessed board, I could ride that fog until dawn.

One last time, Eve. You know you want to.

Oh, how I wanted to listen to that alluring voice and ride above those twisted, dead trees and slanted tombstones until my legs cramped and my back ached. But those carefree days were gone, and the sooner I let them go, the easier it would be to forget. I hurried along—trying to ignore the graveyard, but not having much success—and before I knew it, I was home.

Grandpa's pumpkin-colored sports coach convertible was parked in the driveway, and I rushed inside, because no matter how miserable I felt, Grandpa could always cheer me up. Grandma could, too, but sometimes she wanted to suck my blood, which could get a little uncomfortable at times.

"There's my girl," Grandpa said and threw open his arms. I rushed to him like I did when I was four, like I probably would when I'm forty.

Did I mention Grandpa was a werewolf? And, boy, was he ever ready for the graveyard. He had on his dark sunglasses, his tombstone shorts, flip-flops, and a tee-shirt that read BIG BAD WOLF.

"Hey, Grandma." I gave her a squeeze, and as she sniffed my neck, I pulled away before she got too attracted to my scent. I knew Grandma didn't mean to bite me, but it was like this primal thing she had a hard time controlling, being a vamp and all.

"Looking good, granny," I said, which was an understatement. Grandma was like 250 years old, but since she'd been bitten at twenty-two, well, you could say she didn't look—or act—her age. She wore a black bikini top, which exposed her pierced bellybutton, jean shorts, and blood red heels that placed her about five inches taller than Grandpa.

Grandma lifted her dark shades and perched them on her long blonde hair. Her fangs tugged against her luscious lips as she smiled. "Feeling good, sweetie. *Mmm*, don't you smell good today."

"Uh, thanks."

Dad walked in and ....

Before I continue, I probably should give you some family history.

First off, it wasn't common for a werewolf and a vampire to get married. Back in the old days, they were major enemies, but Grandma and Grandpa—they had broken all sorts of boundaries.

You'd think that with a wolf and a vamp as parents, my dad would've turned out to be one or the other, at least that's what everyone else in Gravesville had thought, but he turned out to be a shapeshifter, which is as unique as they come. Then, there was my mom, a gorgon, purebred and all that. She comes from a long line of gorgons that dated back to like when dates were invented. Gorgons are pretty rare, too. Humans killed off most of them thousands of years ago.

When my parents got together there was this big to-do in Gravesville about what kind of children they would have. And—*hardy-har*—turns out they had a ghoul, my brother Sam, which is like the most common monster next to zombies.

Then, they found me. Okay, I know what you're thinking: Sam's my little brother, so how could he have been born first? Well, ghouls age differently than humans. One year for them equals three years for humans, which really stinks for them because they only celebrate birthdays once every three years.

Anyway, my parents found me at their doorstep, which was a huge problem, because humans are not welcomed in Gravesville. And for good reason! But with me it was different. My parents and grandparents were pretty important monsters, and they managed to convince everyone I should stay. I don't know exactly what they did. Mom and Dad don't like to talk about it, but whatever. Some monsters still look at me funny, and sometimes the younger ones get frightened by my appearance, but that didn't happen so much anymore. Most monsters were used to me.

So where was I? Oh, yeah.

When Dad walked in, he was in his human form, and before Grandpa could get a word in, Dad ran through a list of things my grandparents weren't allowed to do while we were in the human world: no big parties, no bringing home dead carcasses, no howling after midnight, and most of all NO BIG PARTIES. Dad scolded Grandma and Grandpa like a couple of kids, and like a couple of kids they snickered uncontrollably.

When Dad left to finish packing, Grandpa confided in me that they were planning the biggest Halloween party this side of Gravesville, and that it was a shame I would miss it.

If there was a single sound that could've expressed how miserable not being here for Halloween made me feel, it would be a horn, which just so happened to be honking right outside.

"Coach's here!" Mom called out.

My stomach lurched, and I began to feel sick and warm all over.

Time to head to the ship.

Time to leave.

I hugged Grandpa, and then lingered in Grandma's embrace, not because I loved her more, but because I wanted her to bite me so I'd turn into a vamp. That way I could stay here. Grandma must've eaten recently, though. She only sniffed my neck again and told me how delicious I smelled.

I picked up Wolf, and he buried his snout into the crook of my arm. He liked being held, and I got the sense that he was feeling a bit lost and needed to be with someone. I know I did.

Once outside, I gave my old haunted castle a last glance—its beautiful black spires with my ghostly relatives eddying around and waving and blowing kisses, the ravens perched along the parapet. Even the thunderclouds seemed thicker, as if they'd gathered to say goodbye.

Sam trudged back from the graveyard. His head was down, and he appeared so sad and small. He told me how everyone had let him win at Corpse Diving and Shadow Stealing, his two favorite games. I wanted to cry. I knew exactly how he felt.

The coach was shiny black with blood-red curtains and pulled by four skeletal horses. The driver, a ruddy thick goblin with a top hat and gray skin, welcomed everyone, and when he opened his mouth, thick beetles squirmed out and scurried down the inside of his shirt, which made Sam laugh. It was a fun trick for kids, but I was too old for such silliness, though I did offer a little smile. He was, after all, just trying to be nice.

Dad loaded up the coach with our luggage, and we gathered inside. As we pulled away, I heard Grandpa's howl echo throughout the castle.

At least someone would be having fun.

THREE
🕷
THE DEAD LADY

A misty rain swirled around us as we entered Port Carta Marina, a charming seaport made of rich, dark wood that glowed under the gas lamps hanging from the pilings.

Shops of all sorts lined the wharf—places with names like Dead Leg Tavern and Leviathan's Bait & Tackle, which offered rental equipment and a warning: WE WILL NOT BE HELD RESPONSIBLE FOR LOST OR DAMAGED SOULS.

The coach pulled up alongside a colossal midnight black ship with deep-red sails. I craned my neck out the window to get a better view, and saw a half-woman, half-skeleton statue carved into the front of the ship. Above the woman, written in faded cursive, was the name Dead Lady.

Okay, so the ship impressed me, and for a brief moment, I thought the trip wouldn't be so bad, but then I got a closer look at the crew as they busied themselves

25

preparing for our departure ... zombies. Are you kidding me?

The captain, a zombie with swollen blue skin and a big beard of dark green moss, sauntered down the ramp to greet us, his wooden leg clunking against the dock every other step. He wore a dark blue waistcoat with golden buttons and a thick ebony belt with a gaudy brass buckle.

When he flashed a smile, I got a glimpse of his teeth— broken swords piled atop infected gums. He introduced himself as Captain Mossbeard, and he seemed pleasant enough—for a zombie—and he said how pretty I was, even though he grimaced while saying this.

"And look at you. What a strapping young lad. Built like a pirate," the captain said, clapping Sam on the shoulder.

"Really? Did you hear that, Dad?" Sam straightened his crooked back and pressed out his chest. "Built like a pirate."

"You'd make a great one," Dad agreed. "Maybe the captain might even teach you a thing or two about the high seas while we're on this voyage."

"Be delighted to," the captain said and showed off his moldy teeth once more.

Sam couldn't get on the ship quick enough. Me, well, I could wait, though I did have to admit this "voyage," as Dad called it, did sound a little exciting ....

At least until a few days later, when we hit the nastiest storm I'd ever seen, which wouldn't have bothered me so much, if I could see land.

The torrential rain sloshed around the ship while the waves tossed us around. Most of the time, I couldn't tell the difference between sky and ocean. It didn't matter, anyway. Both made me feel as if trapped inside a soaking wet coffin.

Sam, however, was having the time of his life. He and the captain steered the ship while yelling out piratey insults like *scurvy* and *barnacle* to describe their hatred for the storm.

I found shelter in the galley (why didn't they call it a kitchen?) where my mom and dad struggled to keep plates and whatnots from falling off the shelves.

Mom cleaned the broken plates off the floor—the snakes on her head looking pretty seasick as they curled around each other for support—while Dad added two more sets of arms to his human form and tried, with little success, to keep the rest of the dishes and cups from crashing down. With the three of us, we managed to gather most everything not fastened to the wall and lock it away in a sturdy old chest.

The raging storm boomed and cracked, and the galley door crashed open, sending in a blast of wind, which carried the all too familiar smell of the undead.

One of the zombie deckmates stood in the doorway, his clothes dripping wet. He shook some of the water off as his boots squished down the steps. When he saw me, a dreamy grin spread across his face, like he'd just gotten a whiff of the juiciest brain ever.

"Captain be much obliged if you'd relieve some of the hands as they been fighting the storm for hours and are tired and hungry," the zombie said to my dad, though his bloodshot eyes never left me.

"*Arr*," I said, trying on my best pirate voice, and I threw up a hand to salute him.

A tin cup we missed packing rolled off a shelf, and the zombie caught it like he meant for it to happen. He brushed against me as he passed—*Ugh!* I could smell every bit of his wet, dead flesh—and he filled the cup with some green foamy stuff and took a long swig.

"I'll go up. You girls stay here," Dad said.

As good and dry as that sounded, I wasn't into bonding with the brain eater. I'd much rather take my chances with the storm. "I'll go up with you—"

But Mom cut me off. "Listen to your father. It's dangerous out there."

I was going to say, *But Sam's only seven and he's practically driving the ship*, until one of Mom's ill snakes snapped at me. I could tell she wasn't in an arguing mood, so I kept my mouth shut and watched Dad turn into a humongous green gorilla and tromp up the steps and into the storm.

Thankfully, the zombie followed right behind Dad, but my happiness was short lived. Dad must've been big enough for five zombies, because five zombies came down, cursing and stinking. What a bunch of low-life brain eaters they were. Worse, they all smiled as they passed me, and not in a friendly way.

I hadn't noticed the pot simmering on the stove until one of the zombies grabbed it and slammed it down at the center of the table. The others shoved their hands into the slop and scooped out grayish-green jelly and stuffed it into their mouths.

I started to ask Mom if she knew how much longer this storm would last, when I realized she didn't look too good. Her snakes sagged even more than before, and her skin glistened with sweat. "Maybe you should lie down," I said.

"I'll be fine. Just need some air."

She stood up, and for a second I thought her snakes were going to throw up all over the place. Then her cheeks puffed up, and she rushed above deck, leaving me alone with the five hungry zombies and an empty pot of brains.

"Should be over in three hours," One of the zombies said. He kicked his feet up on the table and used a sharp blade to clean a chunk of food from between his teeth.

"Excuse me?" I said, inching backward to create as much distance as I could from the table of brain eaters.

"The storm. It should be over in three hours."

"The storm?" Was that some kind of zombie pirate code for eating my brains? I moved back faster.

"You were asking your mom how long the storm would last. It should be over in three hours."

My back hit a wall, knocking over an old portrait of Captain Mossbeard, one painted before he turned into a zombie. I frantically tried placing the picture frame back on its nail, but I wasn't having much luck.

"Name's John Wart, by the way. I'm the quartermaster. Here, let me see that." He slipped the picture frame onto the nail and checked to make sure it was straight. "And you are?"

"Oh, right. I'm Eve," I managed.

"The mammoth sitting next to me is Sawbones," John Wart continued. "He's the ship's gunner. You need something blown up, he's your zombie."

Sawbones waved at me with a hand the size of a tombstone. "Hi, miss."

The other three zombies were identical triplets, what John Wart called mates. There was Black Feet Pete, Brain Beat Pete and Dead Meat Pete. They each greeted me, speaking at almost the same time and finishing each other's sentence.

"Nice to meet," the first started. "You, Eve. Hope the rough sea," the second continued. "Isn't too much for you," the third finished.

I guess the other zombies had the same problem trying to figure out who was who, because John Wart said, "You can call them Three Petes. It's easier."

During an argument between John Wart and Sawbones over the proper way to barbecue brains, we heard a loud roar from outside followed by what sounded like a mountain crashing into the sea.

Everyone's face at the table turned an unhealthy shade of decay as we waited and listened. At first, I couldn't hear anything except the rain and ocean pounding against the ship, but then the wood below cracked and screamed. Something was tearing into it.

"What's going on?" I demanded.

In answer, the galley door slammed open and a deckhand shouted, "Viperfish just hit the ship!"

FOUR
✦
THE TRIANGLE

After Captain Mossbeard returned from below deck, he reported that the blaggard lass had pillaged so much blasted wood that the only thing keeping his grand and dear ship together was some scally-wagging barnacle.

I was just happy the viperfish hadn't stuck around to finish us off. I'd never seen one before, but I've heard stories about their massive size, spear-like teeth, and soulless eyes. Based on the holes I saw in the walls along the lower deck—my Jack! They were as big as dinner plates!—I had no urge to see a viperfish, either.

We worked as hard as we could to plug up the holes, but it seemed for every bucket we dumped out, a hundred more would pour back in.

It wasn't until seven in the morning that I could finally lay down. My sore feet sloshed in my soaked shoes as I trudged off to bed, and I fell asleep before the blanket hit my chin.

When I woke and stepped outside, I noticed a thick fog blanketing the ship, which under normal circumstances would've been comforting. I walked up to the bridge to see the captain, because I had this odd feeling we were lost.

Captain Mossbeard was steering the ship, as usual, a big, steely grin on his face. I was about to ask him if he knew where we were when I noticed the compass's needle spinning wildly in circles.

"We're lost, aren't we?" I asked.

The captain's rotten lips pulled back in a sneer, showing off his pointy teeth. "We're close," he said. "This is where things start to get interesting, lass."

"Close to what?"

"Why The Triangle of course."

"The Triangle? What's that?" I asked, because in my mind I pictured the ship trying to stuff itself through a triangle-shaped door, which seemed impossible to me.

The captain held his belly and laughed for a long while, giving me more than enough time to feel stupid.

"The Bermuda Triangle. It's the only portal we're allowed to pass through."

Sam ran up the steps and said, "This fog is so thick. I wish we had this stuff back in—" but he cut himself off when his eyes found the spinning needle. "Uh, Captain Mossbeard? I think something's wrong with your compass."

"There's nothing wrong," I said, trying to sound smart with my newfound knowledge. "It means we're almost at the Triangle ... you know, the Bermuda Triangle."

"Is that true?" Sam asked Captain Mossbeard.

"*Aye.* Your sister here was just telling me about the Triangle. I think she might have a little pirate in her after all."

"*Arr,*" I said.

Wow, you're really getting the hang of this pirate thing," Sam beamed.

I whispered *thank you* to the captain, and he winked at me and continued steering his ship through the fog, which was so thick now I could stuff a pillow with it.

Around midday, I went to check on Mom. She had managed to fall asleep, but her normal olive skin was pale and slick with sweat. I refilled the cup of water next to her bed and left her alone.

With nothing else to do, I decided to keep busy by helping Sawbones and Three Petes swab the deck, which seemed suspiciously similiar to mopping. They told me how brave I was with the storm and the viperfish. I didn't think I had been brave. But who was I to argue?

"Good thing the viperfish ... Never showed ... We would've peed ourselves," Three Petes confided to me.

"Only thing worse than a viperfish is a splitter fish," Sawbones said. "Them suckers can multiply by the thousands and rip apart an entire ship within minutes."

"Let's hope we don't run into one of those," I said and shivered at the thought.

"Nah, we'll be through the Triangle 'fore then." Sawbones smiled. Though most of his teeth were black or missing, and he could flatten me with one of his tombstone-sized hands, I couldn't help but find him wonderfully horrible.

Before long, swabbing became too much like work, and I pretended to be a pirate, which was much more fun. I *arred* and *yo hoed* and *barnacled* this and *avasted* that.

Sawbones and Three Petes joined in by pretending to be humans. Sawbones put the business end of a mop on his head and brushed the mop-hair out of his eyes like a human damsel in distress.

"Oh, who will save me? I'm a silly human, and I don't know how to think without help."

Three Petes attempted to rescue him—um, her—but when they tried to pick Sawbones up, who easily weighed as much as the triplets put together, they all collapsed to the deck, and I laughed so hard tears ran down my cheeks.

"Are these bilge-sucking sea scum giving you a hard time, lass?" Captain Mossbeard asked. His smile told me he didn't mind us goofing off.

"*Arr*, they should walk the plank to Danny Jones' cabin," I said with a sharp salute.

"Don't you mean Davy Jones' locker?"

"*Arr*," I said.

"You better stay on this one's good side," the captain said to his crew. "She has even less patience than I do with you scalleywags. He laughed heartily and then added, "Wanted to let you know we'll be passing through the Triangle soon. It be good to get your mom up. Fresh sun and salt on the other side should fix her right up."

I guess he saw the concern on my face, because he asked, "What's wrong, lass?"

"Did you say it's gonna be sunny on the other side?" I asked. In Gravesville there was no sun, only darkness at night and heavy fog and thunderclouds during the day. Occasionally something that might be the sun reddened the clouds to puffy bruises, and of course we had a big and beautiful moon and stars, but pure sunlight ...?

"My friend Sally once told me that if the sun were ever to break through the clouds, we'd all melt."

When the captain stopped laughing, he said, "I'm sorry, lass. I've been on the sea far too long. It's not every day I meet someone who's never seen the sun."

I shrugged. "I've never been outside of Gravesville before."

"Well then, I would humbly request that you join me on the bridge when we cross through the Triangle. You won't be disappointed."

"But what about melting?"

"You're a human, and we're going to a world of humans that haven't melted yet. I think you'll be fine."

I went below deck to check on Mom and to ask her about this whole sun thing, but she was still asleep. I couldn't find my dad, either. I figured he was sleeping, too, especially after all the work he'd done to help close up the holes in the ship.

I recalled something else Sally had told me about the sun. That it was about 11,000 degrees, which seemed pretty hot to me. I know the captain had said that all those other humans haven't melted, but maybe those humans had adapted to the sun over time. Maybe their skin was thicker than mine.

Not taking any chances, I put on as many clothes as my body could hold: a wool hat, a scarf wrapped three times around my neck, wool gloves, a long-buttoned shirt, black cotton pants, two pairs of socks, my black snow boots, and a heavy overcoat with a soft, furry hood. I didn't want my eyes to melt, either, so I grabbed a pair of sunglasses, the ones my mom used when she didn't feel like wearing her special contacts.

"I'm ready for you, sun," I announced into a mirror.

A few minutes later, a deckhand came down and told me that the captain requested my presence on the bridge, and that we would be crossing over into the Triangle at any moment.

I had never been more scared in my life.

The ship was eerily quiet as I pushed through the fog and made my way to the bridge.

When Captain Mossbeard saw me bundled up for the sun, his mouth opened and shut as if he were about to say something but thought better of it. Instead, he shook his head and walked to the railing to address his crew.

"Triangle dead ahead! Batten down the hatches! Hoist the main sails. Jimmy that rig, maggots!"

Suddenly, howling wind blasted my face and cut into the snapping sails. I could feel myself tipping backward as water gushed from beneath the ship.

"We're falling, lass. Grab onto something. It's about to get bumpy," the captain said, spinning the ship's wheel this way and that.

FIVE

🕷

INTO THE NEW WORLD

My legs lifted from the deck, and I felt my grip slipping as the ship pitched down into the misty unknown.

"Hold on, lass! Almost there!" the captain yelled, but I could barely hear him over the screaming deckhands and roaring wind.

The ship plunged into the ocean, sending a huge wave crashing over the bow, dousing everything and everyone. For a moment, I thought we were going to sink, but then the bow surged up from the water, and the ship lurched from side to side as sheets of ankle-high water swirled around the deck.

Sam rushed up to the bridge. "That was awesome! Can we do it again?"

I used the railing to pull myself up as the ship settled into the smooth rhythm of the sea. My legs wobbled, probably from the extra twenty pounds of soaked layers I wore.

"You need help," I managed.

My attention soon shifted to a single beam of golden light that pierced through the fog right in front of me.

"Is that ...?"

"Sunlight," the captain said. "Go ahead, lass, touch it."

Though part of me expected the light to burn a hole right through my hand, I couldn't help myself. It was too wondrous.

Oh, how amazingly warm the light felt—like holding a rare and perfect jewel— and I wanted to keep it with me always and learn its mysteries.

Another beam of light burst through the fog. Then another. The radiant beams expanded, burning away the fog until the sky opened up to a clear blue, and then the light seemed to break apart and scatter into the water, which sparkled all around us.

Captain Mossbeard turned me around. "Look, lass. There she be."

I cupped my hand over my eyes and peered at the flaming ball that sat on the edge of this new world.

And I cried.

"It's amazing," I said to the captain. "I never would've imagined ..."

Sam wasn't as excited as me. "I'd rather the thunderclouds, maybe some lightning. This is boring. And it's hot! I'm going below to get a drink."

I pulled off my hat and gloves first, because it was hot out here. As I took off my jacket and scarf, I saw Dad assisting Mom up the steps, and I rushed over to them.

"Isn't this amazing, Mom! If this doesn't make you feel better, I don't know what will."

"It's beautiful," Mom agreed as she sat down on an old crate full of ropes. She was still weak, but her snakes seemed to have made a full recovery. They bobbed and swayed with tongues flicking as they explored this new world.

By the next morning, Mom's sickness had passed. I would've been happier, too, if the sun hadn't fried my skin. I could barely move. I had an even harder time trying to sleep. About the only thing I could do over the next few days was curse the sun for its wickedness.

Wolf stayed by my side, and Mom and Dad came to check in on me every once in a while, but there wasn't much they could do. The captain even stopped by to cheer me up. He told me he'd heard of such burns caused by the sun, but the pain should pass, though he was pretty sure I'd start shedding skin like a snake soon.

The pain did go away after a few days, and the shedding, while adorably itchy, wasn't as bad as the captain had made it sound. I still hated that sinister fireball, and more than ever I wanted to go home, so on the ninth day of our voyage, I marched up to the bridge and demanded Captain Mossbeard to turn this ship around. When that didn't work, I begged him.

"Sorry, lass, but we be arriving late tomorrow evening, whether you like it or not. But you'll be happy to know I got something special planned for you and yer family. That should cheer you up some."

For our final night aboard the Dead Lady, the captain threw us a feast on the main deck of the ship. The crew drank mugs of gray frothy ale and ate pot after pot of fresh brains, while my family and I opted for the chocolate chip muffins dripping with caramel butter, plates of fried dough dipped in sugar and tall mugs full of spiced pumpkin cider, which Three Petes had made themselves.

While we ate, Captain Mossbeard stood and knocked his wooden leg against the floorboard to get everyone's attention. "Settle down, maggots. It's time for a toast." The captain raised his glass, and we all did the same. "To a fine family. May the wind always be at your back, and the stars find you home safely. Here's to the Hallows, who I will forever call friends."

Dad thanked the captain and crew for all their hard work in getting us to the human world, while Mom thanked everyone for helping her through her illness. Sam and I even got into the spirit, and soon thank yous were being tossed around by everyone.

"And I have a special surprise for you two," Captain Mossbeard said to Sam and me. "Meet me on the bridge in ten minutes."

Sawbones and Three Petes snickered, and John Wart nudged me with his forearm and said, "You're gonna love it. Made it myself."

"What do you think it is?" Sam asked. "I bet it's a sword ... or an eye patch ... or a pirate flag ... or buried treasure!"

"Buried treasure. Now that's the best kind of treasure," John Wart said, and the deckhands cheered and raised their mugs.

After our ten-minute wait was up, Sam and I rushed up to the bridge, and the captain handed Sam his present first.

"Oh, it's horrible!" Sam exclaimed. He pulled out a curved sword with silver skull patterns woven into the handle.

"Now, you're a real pirate," the captain said and clapped a hand on Sam's back.

"And I didn't forget about you, lass." He plucked a small rectangular box from his waistcoat and handed it to me.

When I slid open the lid, my jaw nearly plinked to the floor. It was the most horrible necklace I had ever seen!

I ran my fingers over the stones, and they began to glow, changing colors from blue to green to red to purple to orange.

"Let me help you put it on," John Wart said, and I lifted my hair so he could clasp the necklace around my neck.

I couldn't stop touching the stones. Not only did they glow and change colors, but they were also so smooth, and they shifted from cool to warm, giving me goosebumps, and then melting them away.

"I've never seen stones like this."

"Not stones, lass," Captain Mossbeard corrected, "fairy hearts."

"I had no ideas fairies even existed," I said.

The captain gave me an odd smile, more of a sneer, really. "Rare and beautiful stones for a rare and beautiful girl."

The party continued for hours. I was having such a great time dancing and singing pirate songs, I didn't want the night to end, but Mom thought otherwise and sent Sam and me off to bed, using the excuse that we had a long day tomorrow.

While cozy under my blanket, I listened to the ocean lap against the side of the ship and soon fell into a deep, comfortable sleep.

My brother poked me in the face some time later.

"Wake up, Eve. We're here."

"Where's here?" I managed, rubbing my eyes and stretching out my legs.

"New Jersey." Sam peeked through the porthole above me. "Hmm, doesn't look all that *new* to me."

ABOUT THE AUTHOR

Robert Gray is a writer. If that job description doesn't impress you, how about fantasy writer? Too general? Well, he doesn't get insulted if you call him a horror writer. If horror's not your thing, then scratch out horror and replace it with suspense. And for the kiddies, you can slap on a YA or MG in front of that title.

Gray lives in Bushkill, Pennsylvania with his wife and two children.

You can communicate with him online at these fine locations:
Facebook: https://www.facebook.com/robertgrayfiction
Twitter: http://twitter.com/rgrayfiction
Blogger: http://robertgrayfiction.blogspot.com/
Email: EveHallows1031@gmail.com

Made in the USA
Charleston, SC
08 August 2011